A Note to the Reader

My older sister took me to see Walt Disney's animated film *Bambi* in 1942 when it was first shown, and I laughed and cried and was dazzled by it as every child is. But it was not until I was grown-up that I discovered the book by Felix Salten on which Walt Disney based his now classic film. Reading it moved and dazzled me even more.

The original book carried the subtitle *A Life in the Woods*, and it was perhaps the first ecological novel. Salten wrote with the heart of a poet, and though he gave voices to the animals and even leaves on the trees, he was true to nature, true to animal behaviour. He presents not only the beauty of the natural world but its harshness as well, and raises provocative questions about the role of man – questions that the movie fails to touch.

Salten, who was born in 1869 in Budapest and died in 1945 in Vienna where he lived most of his life, wrote *Bambi* in German. It was first published in 1923 in Berlin. The first American edition, with Whittaker Chamber's skilful translation into English, appeared in 1928. In writing my storybook adaptation I have used for the most part the actual sentences of Salten's lyrical prose and have tried to retain his spirit and purpose, though, of course, the narrative has been greatly shortened.

It is my hope that young animal lovers will discover the true Bambi and his world in this beautifully illustrated storybook and then one day go on to read Salten's full-length masterpiece.

Janet Schulman
October 1999

For Susanne and Stig
– J. S.

For our firstborn
– S. J. & L. F.

Felix Salten's
BAMBI

Adaptation of the original story by Janet Schulman
Paintings by Steve Johnson and Lou Fancher

Simon & Schuster
London   New York   Sydney

He was born in the middle of the forest in one of those little hidden glades. He stood there, swaying unsteadily on his thin legs.

"What a beautiful child," cried the magpie, perched on a dogwood branch. "How amazing to think that he should be able to get right up and walk! Can he run too?"

"Of course," replied the mother softly, interrupting her washing of her newly born for a moment. She washed him with her tongue, smoothing his tousled red coat with its fine white spots.

Though the forest was alive with the early morning call of birds, the little fawn understood not one word of their conversations. Nor did he smell the rich aroma of the woods. He heard only the soft licking that washed and warmed him, and he smelled nothing but his mother's body near him. She smelled good, and he snuggled up closer to her. "Bambi," she whispered. "My little Bambi."

During the first few weeks of Bambi's life he stayed with his mother in the hidden glade and followed behind her on narrow tracks that ran through thick foliage. He was curious about everything and asked his mother many questions. He learned that he was a little deer and his mother a big deer, that the trails through the forest were made by the deer.

Once, when he saw a ferret pounce upon a mouse and kill it, Bambi asked his mother anxiously, "Shall we kill a mouse too, sometime?" And then he learned that deer never kill anything.

Another day he heard two jays quarrelling. "Mother," he asked, "will we be angry with each other sometime and scream at each other, like those birds?"

"No, child," said his mother, "we deer don't do such things."

Then at dawn one fine morning the trail they followed led to a bright open meadow. Bambi wanted to bound forward, but his mother stopped him. She explained that walking on the meadow is dangerous and that certain rules must always be followed.

"Now do exactly as I tell you," she said. "I'm going out alone first. Stay here and wait. And don't take your eyes off me for a minute. If you see me run back, then turn around and run as fast as you can." She grew silent and seemed to be thinking before she continued her instructions to Bambi. "Run even if you should see me fall to the ground. Don't think of me, do you understand? Just run. Do you promise to do that?"

"Yes," said Bambi softly. His mother spoke so seriously.

She walked slowly out onto the meadow. Bambi saw how she looked all about and took slow, cautious steps. Finally she called to him, "Come!"

**B**ambi bounded out. Joy seized him. For the first time he could see the whole blue sky stretching above him and feel the hot, blinding sunlight all around. He leaped into the air over and over again.

But Bambi did not understand how to run freely around the open field until his mother laughingly said, "Catch me!" And in a flash she was off, with Bambi chasing after her. Around and around the meadow they went. The swishing grass sounded wonderful to Bambi's ears and he drank in the sweet air. Suddenly the race was over, and they began strolling contentedly side by side.

Then Bambi began enjoying the meadow with his eyes also. The broad green field was sprinkled with white daisies, purple clover blossoms and bright golden dandelions.

"Look, Mother!" he exclaimed. "There's a flower flying."

"That's not a flower," said his mother, smiling. "That's a butterfly."

"Look," cried Bambi, "see that piece of grass jumping."

"That's not grass," his mother explained. "That's a grasshopper, and he

hopped that way because he was afraid that we'd step on him."

Bambi walked over to the daisy on which the grasshopper had jumped. "Excuse us for disturbing you," said Bambi shyly.

"Since it's you, it's perfectly all right," said the grasshopper. "And now you must excuse me. I have to be looking for my wife, Hopp." And he gave a jump and vanished in the grass.

"Mother, I spoke to the grasshopper!" said Bambi. He was excited. It was the first time he had ever spoken to a stranger.

He noticed a butterfly sitting on a grass stem and fanning its wings slowly. Bambi moved toward it and said, "Oh, how beautiful you are, as beautiful as a flower."

"What?" cried the butterfly. "In my circle it's generally supposed that we're handsomer than flowers." Then the insulted butterfly fluttered off.

And that was how Bambi found the meadow on his very first visit.

The next day Bambi did not want to sleep in their snug little glade. He was wide awake and longed to play again on the meadow. His mother was dozing in the midday heat when Bambi nudged her. "Come on," he begged. "Let's go to the meadow."

His mother lifted her head. "Now? Certainly not!" she said, her voice full of astonishment and terror. "Why, it's broad daylight."

"But it was broad daylight when we went before," Bambi objected.

"It was early in the morning," she said. "We can only go to the meadow in the early morning or late evening. Or at night. It is too dangerous any other time."

"Why is it dangerous?" asked Bambi, all attention.

His mother did not want to continue the conversation. "You are too young to understand. Now lie down and go to sleep until evening. We're safe here."

But Bambi did not want to sleep. "Why are we safe here?" he asked.

"Because the bushes hide us," his mother answered, "and last year's dead leaves rustle to warn us, and the jays and magpies keep watch to tell us if anybody is coming."

"What are last year's leaves?" Bambi asked.

"Come and sit beside me," said his mother, "and I will tell you." And she told him how when it grows cold the leaves turn yellow, brown and red and fall slowly until the trees look perfectly naked. But the dry leaves lie on the ground and when a foot stirs them they rustle. Then the deer know someone is coming. "Oh, how kind last year's dead leaves are!" she said.

Bambi pressed close against his mother as he listened to her. When she grew silent he began to think about the kind leaves. He wondered just what that terrible danger she didn't want to talk about could be. Then he fell asleep.

That evening when Bambi and his mother were playing tag in the meadow, his mother saw her friend the hare and introduced him to Bambi.

"Good evening, young man," said Hare politely.

Bambi thought the hare's long spoonlike ears, which at times stood bolt upright and at others fell back limply as though they had suddenly grown weak, were funny. Bambi had to laugh.

The hare laughed quickly too, but then his eyes grew more thoughtful. To Bambi's surprise he suddenly sat straight up on his hind legs and said to Bambi's mother, "What a charming young prince. I sincerely congratulate you. Yes, indeed, he'll make a splendid prince in time." And with that, the hare excused himself – "I have all kinds of things to do tonight" – and hopped off, ears back, so they touched his shoulders.

His mother smiled. "The good hare. He doesn't have an easy time of it in this world," she said sympathetically as she put her head deep into the sweet grass.

Bambi left his mother to her meal, and strolled about. Just as he was wishing that all the creatures he met didn't have to rush off, he noticed something – no, two somethings – moving in the tall grass on the far side of the meadow. Then he saw a creature that looked just like his mother.

"Mother, look, over there!" Bambi called.

She raised her head and smiled. "Why, it's my sister, Ena, and she has had two babies! Just think, two of them! Come, Bambi, let's go and meet them."

**B**ambi's mother introduced him to his Aunt Ena, who said, "And this is Gobo and Faline. Now, children, you run along and play together."

That is exactly what Bambi wanted to do, but the three children were all a little shy. They stared at each other for a moment. No one said a word. Then suddenly Faline gave a leap and rushed about. In a moment Bambi darted after her and Faline's brother, Gobo, followed. They flew around in circles, they turned tail and fell over each other, they chased each other up and down. It was glorious. And when they finally stopped, all out of breath, they were already good friends.

Every day from then on the three young deer played together in the meadow,

and when they were tired of chasing back and forth they stopped and chattered to each other endlessly.

One day after Gobo had told Bambi about his encounter with an unfriendly hedgehog, Bambi grew quiet. After a moment he softly asked Gobo and Faline, "Do you know what 'danger' means?"

"Danger," whispered Gobo, "is something very bad."

"Yes," said Bambi, "I know that, but what *is* it?"

All three trembled with fear until Faline could no longer bear staying there and being frightened. "I know what danger is – it's what you run away from," she cried loudly, and sprang away. In an instant Bambi and Gobo bounded after her and they began to chase and play again.

Then just as their mothers were calling, "Come, it's time to go home," two huge creatures came crashing out of the woods. They tore by like the wind and then vanished into the woods again. In a few moments they came bursting out of the thicket and walked regally past the children in silent splendour before disappearing finally.

Bambi stared after them in awe. They had looked like his mother and Aunt Ena, but their heads were crowned with gleaming antlers.

"Who were they?" cried Faline excitedly.

"Who were they?" Gobo repeated in a hardly audible voice.

Bambi kept silent.

Aunt Ena said solemnly, "Those were your fathers."

On the trail home Bambi was unusually quiet.

As though his mother could read his thoughts, she said, "If you are cunning, my son, and don't run into danger, you'll be as strong and handsome as your father, and you'll have antlers like his too."

Bambi's heart swelled with joy.

ime passed and Bambi had many adventures. He learned how to listen intelligently to everything that stirred, to pick out the softest sound – even the sound field mice make as they run to and fro. He learned how to sniff the air now too: when the wind blew off the fields he could tell if Friend Hare was out there or if a fox had trotted by recently. And, of course, Bambi made many new friends. He especially admired the old owl who flew without a sound even though she was so very big. And though Bambi didn't understand most of the clever things she said, he knew that they were clever and he greatly respected her. The much smaller, playful screech owl was always delighted when his terrible, high-pitched screeches caught someone unawares and made them jump. This happened to Bambi the first few times he met the little owl. After that Bambi would pretend to be frightened. It pleased the screech owl so much.

Every day brought some new experience. The first time a raging storm broke over the forest, when the midday sky grew dark and lightning flashed and thunder crashed, Bambi was numb with fear. He thought the end of the world had come.

And the first time he woke to
find his mother gone from his side,
he was frightened also. He wandered
off, calling mournfully, "Mother! Mother!"
Then, in the middle of a clearing, he stopped
short as if frozen to the ground.

By the edge a strange creature was standing.
Bambi had never seen such a creature before. It had
a smell that was unpleasant and sharp and filled
him with terror. He stared at the creature, which
stood remarkably erect on its hind legs and had
a pale face without fur.

Suddenly it stretched out a leg from high up
near its face. Bambi had not even noticed that a leg
was there! The mere gesture of the leg moving out
into the air set Bambi in motion. In a flash he was
back in the thicket and running.

A moment later his mother was beside him.
Together they bounded over shrubs and bushes and
did not stop running until they came to their glade.

"Did you see Him?" asked Bambi's mother softly.

Bambi had no breath left. He could only nod yes.

"That was He," she said.

And they both shuddered.

**B**ambi was often alone now. "You aren't a little baby anymore," his mother would say, sometimes impatiently, as she went off by herself. He was getting used to being on his own, but one night as he wandered for hours he simply couldn't bear to be so utterly alone anymore. He began to call for his mother.

Suddenly one of the stags was blocking the trail, looking sternly down at him. Standing in a pool of moonlight, this stag looked more powerful and taller and prouder than any Bambi had ever seen. His coat was a deep rich red,

but his face was flecked with silvery grey, and on his head was a high, wide crown of black, beaded antlers.

"What are you crying about?" the old stag asked severely. Bambi trembled in awe and did not dare answer. "Can't you stay by yourself? Shame on you!" And then the stag disappeared as suddenly as he had appeared.

"He spoke to you!" said a soft voice that made Bambi jump. The hare hopped out into the moonlight.

"Oh, Friend Hare, did you see him?" asked Bambi. "Who is he?"

The hare hopped closer to Bambi. "He is the biggest and the oldest stag in the whole forest," said Hare. "It is said he speaks to no one, but that cannot be true. . . ."

Bambi begged the hare to tell him more.

"Nobody knows where he lives," continued Hare. "Very few have seen him even once. At times he was thought to be dead because he hadn't been seen for so long. He knows the very depths of the forest. Other princes fight one another at times, but for many years no one has fought with the old stag. And of those who fought with him long ago not one is living. He does not know such a thing as danger. No one dares speak to him. He is the Great Prince."

"Oh, he is wonderful," said Bambi. "I wanted so to speak to him, but I was afraid. If I ever see him again, I will."

The hare studied Bambi for a moment and then said, "Yes, perhaps you will. And now, young prince, I must be off."

week passed and then a terrible event happened. As dawn broke over the meadow, Bambi was standing near a handsome stag by the big oak. He was gathering his courage to speak, when there was a crash like thunder. The stag jumped grotesquely into the air and in one great bound was in the woods. In an instant Bambi's mother, Aunt Ena, and Gobo and Faline, who were grazing on the other side of the meadow, fled in terror. Bambi had made only a few bounds into the thicket when he saw the stag lying on the ground. He was dead.

"Don't stop!" a voice beside him commanded. It was his mother, who rushed past him at full gallop. "Run as fast as you can."

Bambi ran after her with all his might, calling, "What is it, Mother?"

His mother answered between gasps, "It . . . was . . . He!"

At last they stopped for lack of breath. A squirrel came chattering through the branches above them. "I ran the whole way with you," he cried. "It was dreadful. I am still trembling."

"I'm quite weak from fright myself," said Bambi's mother. "I don't understand it. Not one of us saw a thing."

"Well, I saw Him long before," said the squirrel. "I tried to warn the prince."

"So did I," cried a magpie. "I called and called, but he was too proud to listen."

"And I," rasped a jay. "How often did I scream, but he was too stupid."

"No," said a crow seriously, "the prince did not die because he was proud or stupid, but because no one can escape Him."

**B**ambi looked around. His mother was no longer there. He wanted to ask her, "Who is this 'He' they talk about?" Bambi was troubled. He thought of the handsome prince lying dead in front of him. He remembered how silent the woods had become an instant after the crash rang out. But already the forest was singing with a thousand voices; far above the falcons were calling, and close at hand a woodpecker hammered as if nothing had happened. He did not understand how the others could be so carefree and happy while life was so difficult and dangerous.

Bambi walked deeper and deeper into the woods. He wanted to find some hiding place where he could never be seen.

Something moved very softly in the bushes and the Great Prince stepped out in front of Bambi. The young deer trembled and wanted to run away, but he controlled himself. "Were you out there on the meadow when it happened?" the old stag asked him.

"Yes," Bambi said softly, his heart pounding in his throat.

"And you're not calling for your mother?"

Bambi looked into the noble face and suddenly felt full of courage. "I can stay by myself now. I haven't cried since you scolded me, Prince." The stag looked at Bambi appraisingly and smiled ever so slightly. "Noble Prince," Bambi continued with newfound confidence, "what has happened? Who is this 'He' they are all talking about?"

The old stag gazed past Bambi into the distance. Then he said slowly, "Listen, smell and see for yourself. Live by yourself. Find out for yourself." He lifted his antlered head still higher. "Farewell." Then he vanished into the depths of the forest.

Bambi stood transfixed. "Farewell," the old stag had said, so he couldn't have been angry. Bambi felt himself thrill with pride, inspired by the Great Prince. Yes, life was difficult and full of danger. But come what might, he would learn to bear it all.

**W**inter soon came and with it bitter cold and little food. The snow, which at first had delighted Bambi, became the great enemy. He had to paw it away before he could find a few withered blades of grass, and often the snow crust would cut his legs. He was always hungry and cold.

The deer were together more now and were much more friendly. Even some of the princes would join them from time to time. Bambi admired Prince Ronno, and he longed to be good friends with handsome young Karus. Bambi loved to listen to the stories the grown-ups told. He heard more about Him than ever before.

"He has three hands, but not always," said young Karus. "My friend the crow, who is very well informed, told me that the third hand is the bad one. It isn't attached like the other two, but He carries it hanging over His shoulder. If He comes without the third hand He isn't dangerous."

"He throws His hand at you, my grandmother told me so," said Bambi's mother. "Then the fire flashes and the thunder cracks. He's all fire inside."

"It's true that He's all fire inside," said Ronno. "But a hand couldn't make such wounds. It is much more likely that it's a tooth He throws at us. You really die from His bite."

And so the winter dragged on with endless rumours and discussions about Him to help take their minds off their hunger and cold. Of all the deer, Gobo felt the harshness of winter the most. He had always been smaller and more delicate than Bambi or Faline. Now he shivered constantly and was so weak that he could hardly stand up.

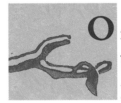 **O**ne day the crows began calling and then a whole flock flapped by, followed in a moment by three jays screaming, "Look out! Look out!"

The deer stood still, sniffing the air. A heavy wave of scent blew past. It filled their nostrils; it numbed their senses and made their hearts stop beating. It was He. And this time the scent was so overpowering that they knew He had come with many others.

Friend Hare hopped up, gasping for breath. "We are surrounded," he said. "He is everywhere!"

At the same instant they heard His voice, twenty or thirty strong, and the snapping and cracking of twigs and boughs as He came closer and closer to the heart of the thicket. A pheasant rose from under His very feet. There was a single crash like thunder and the pheasant fell from the sky.

Suddenly all sorts of creatures were swarming past the deer – a pair of weasels, a ferret, squirrels, a fox, even tiny titmice.

"Don't try to fly," shouted a pheasant to the others. "Just run! Don't lose your head! Don't try to fly!" But then the poor bird panicked. As he flew upward, a short crash like thunder sounded sharply and he fell from the sky. Then all the pheasants lost their senses and tried to fly away. The crashing thunder started in earnest. *Bang! Bang! Bang!*

"Bambi, my child," said his mother. "We must get out of here. Keep behind me. Don't run. But when we have to cross the open place, run as fast as you can. And don't forget, even if I fall, just keep running."

His mother walked carefully amidst the uproar. They could see the clearing up ahead through the naked bushes. Then Bambi heard steps and looked around. The dreaded He was there, bursting through the bushes on all sides!

"Now!" said Bambi's mother, and she was off with a bound that barely skimmed the snow. Bambi rushed after her. The thunder crashed around them. Bambi saw nothing. He just kept running.

The open space was crossed. Another thicket took him in. He looked around for his mother but did not see her. He kept running even though the thunder grew more distant. He stopped with a jolt when he heard another deer cry, "Is that you, Bambi?"

Bambi saw Gobo lying helplessly in the snow. "Get up, Gobo! There's not a moment to lose," cried Bambi. "Where's your mother and Faline?"

"They had to leave me here," said Gobo. "I fell down. I can't stand up. I'm too weak. Go on, Bambi." The uproar began again with new crashes of thunder coming nearer.

Suddenly young Karus pounded by. When he saw Bambi and Gobo he called to them, "Run! Don't stand there if you can run!" He was gone in a flash and his flight carried Bambi along with it. Bambi was hardly aware that he had begun to run again, and he called softly behind him, "Good-bye, Gobo."

Bambi ran until darkness closed in and the forest grew quiet. The first friend whom Bambi saw again was Ronno. "Have you seen my mother?" Bambi asked him.

"No," answered Ronno, and walked quickly away as though he did not want to discuss it further.

Later Bambi saw Faline, who explained that her mother had gone back to try to find Gobo. Bambi told how he had seen Gobo, and they grew so sad that both were crying when Aunt Ena returned.

"My poor little Gobo is gone," she cried. "I went to the place where he lay in the snow, but there was no trace of him, not even his tracks . . . just big tracks, His tracks. He took my Gobo."

She was silent. Then Bambi asked, "Aunt Ena, have you seen my mother?"

"No," answered Aunt Ena gently.

Bambi never saw his mother again.

At last the trees began turning green. Spring had arrived and with it a pair of wonderful antlers on Bambi's head.

He was intently pounding them against a tree to get rid of the skin that still covered them when the chatty squirrel who lived in the big oak on the meadow came scurrying near. "Well, you are nearly grown now," said the squirrel, "and you are going to be a remarkably handsome prince with such long bright prongs to your antlers. You don't often see the like."

"Really?" Bambi said, and was so delighted that he immediately began pounding the tree harder.

Bambi missed his mother terribly; he also missed Gobo, and he seldom saw Faline. She seemed to have grown unusually shy. The older bucks chased Bambi whenever they saw him. Ronno treated him worst of all. He found a place deep in the forest, far from the glade where he had lived with his mother. It was a lonely time for Bambi.

Then one hot, still evening, as spring turned into summer, a longing stirred Bambi to wander far afield. Quite unexpectedly he met Faline. He stared at her speechless for a moment and then said, "Oh, how beautiful you have grown, Faline!"

Faline smiled. "It's a long time since we've seen each other," she said in her familiar bantering tone.

They began talking of old times and asked each other every minute, "Do you remember?" And they were both pleased that each still remembered everything.

"Do you remember how we used to play tag in the meadow?" Bambi asked.

"Yes, it was like this," said Faline, and she was off like an arrow with Bambi joyously after her.

From then on Bambi and Faline were often together. They had such fun and understood each other perfectly.

Once as Bambi was going to meet Faline, he heard her shrill call of distress and fear. He ran quickly to the meadow where he saw Ronno pursuing her as she fled into the thicket.

"Leave Faline alone," Bambi warned Ronno.

"Our little Bambi thinks he can tell me what to do!" said Ronno scornfully. "Have you forgotten how often I've chased you?"

Bambi was furious. He would no longer be treated as a child! He tore at Ronno and smashed into him with a crash that sent Ronno reeling. Before he could recover, Bambi was at him again, ripping open Ronno's shoulder.

"Let me go," Ronno groaned, but Bambi had no thoughts of mercy. As Bambi was preparing to charge once more, Ronno whined, "Please stop! Can't you take a joke?"

Bambi left him alone and Ronno slunk off in silence. In a moment Faline leaped out of the thicket and ran over to Bambi.

"That was wonderful," she said laughingly. Then she added softly and seriously, "I love you."

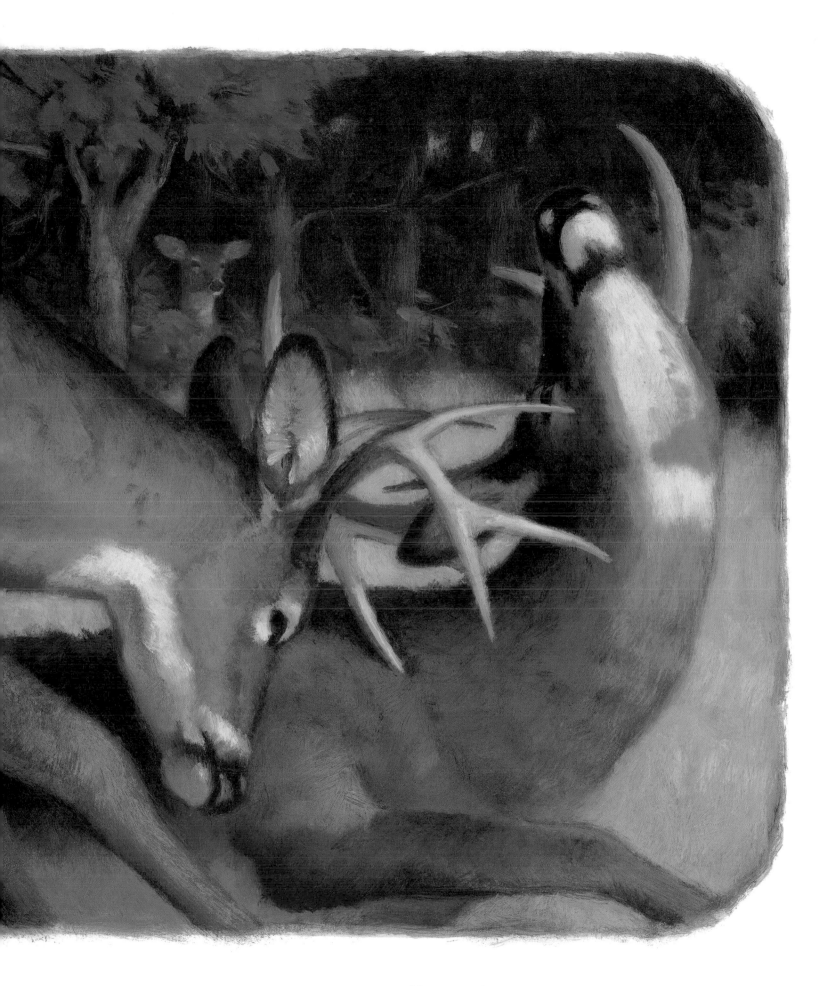

A few days later they saw a new deer on the meadow. He was a young buck with small antlers and his coat was sleek and very red. Bambi and Faline had never seen such a fat deer, nor one who acted so carelessly, never sniffing the air or looking about for danger.

The stranger was busy nibbling the grass and did not notice Bambi and Faline until they were almost on top of him. When he saw them he ran to them in childish little skips and called joyfully, "Faline! Bambi! Don't you know me?"

Suddenly Faline rushed to the stranger. "Gobo!" she cried, and stood there speechless.

"Faline," said Gobo softly. He kissed his sister. Tears were running down his cheeks. Faline was crying too.

"Well, Gobo," said Bambi, thoroughly bewildered. "So you're not dead. Where have you been all this time?"

"With Him," Gobo replied proudly. Bambi's and Faline's astonishment amused Gobo. "Yes, my dears, I've seen a lot more than all of you put together in your old forest."

"Tell us about it," cried Faline, beside herself with joy that her brother had returned to them.

"I will, I will, but first I want to find Mother," said Gobo, and then he asked softly, "She is still alive?"

"Yes," said Faline. "I haven't seen her for a long while, but we can find her together."

It took the three of them most of the day to find her, and what a joyous reunion there was! Ena did not ask any questions. She simply kissed Gobo tirelessly, as she had when he was born.

That evening they all gathered in a little clearing near the meadow to hear Gobo's story. Even Friend Hare was there and would lift one spoonlike ear in astonishment from time to time. The magpie, perched on the lowest branch of a beech, listened in amazement. The jay let out a scream every once in a while in wonder. The squirrel kept scurrying from one tree to another, wild with excitement and forever trying to interrupt with his own tale about a squirrel who had been shut up with Him for a week.

obo explained how dogs had found him lying in the snow and barked terribly, so that he thought his heart would stop. But then He came and carried Gobo to the place where He lived.

"Outside this place it is all snow and howling cold, but inside it's as warm as summer. And the rain can pour outside, but inside it is dry and cosy," he said. "There is always plenty to eat. He gave me hay and chestnuts, potatoes and turnips – whatever I wanted," boasted Gobo.

"Weren't you ever afraid, Gobo?" asked Faline.

"No, dear Faline," he said. "I got to know that He wouldn't hurt me. He is all powerful, but if He loves you or if you serve Him, He's good to you. Nobody in the world can be as kind as He can. Not only He, but all His children loved me. They used to pet me and play with me."

While Gobo was talking the Great Prince suddenly stepped from the bushes. Gobo didn't notice him and went on talking, but the others saw the old stag and held their breath in awe.

Finally the Great Prince asked in his quiet, commanding voice, "What kind of band is that you have on your neck?"

"Why, that's part of the halter I wore," stammered Gobo uneasily. "It's the greatest honour to wear His halter, it's . . ." Gobo trailed off.

Everyone was silent. The old stag looked at Gobo for a long time, piercingly and sadly. "You poor thing!" he said softly, then turned and was gone.

**E**veryone soon saw that Gobo had habits that seemed strange to the rest of them. He slept at night when the others were awake, and would go out on the meadow in the noonday sun without any hesitation. "Don't you ever think of the danger?" Bambi asked Gobo.

"No," Gobo said, "there isn't any for me. He is my friend. And when winter comes, if it gets too hard for me, I'll simply go back to Him."

A few days later, when the birds sounded their warning calls, all the animals fled for cover – except Gobo. One sharp *bang* sounded across the meadow and Gobo fell.

Bambi had seen Him raise His third arm and kill poor foolish Gobo. It troubled Bambi greatly and he thought about it for weeks. He thought about what the wise old stag had told him: live by yourself; find out for yourself.

There was a chill in the air now and the foliage was turning gold and red. Bambi was almost always by himself, but one night he met Faline.

She looked sadly at him and shyly said, "I'm so much alone now."

"I'm alone too," Bambi answered, avoiding her eyes.

"Why don't you stay with me anymore? Do you still love me?" she asked sorrowfully.

It hurt Bambi to see Faline so downcast. Finally he replied, "I don't know. I just want to be alone." He tried to say it gently, but he knew it sounded hard.

Faline walked silently away from him, and all at once Bambi felt a great weight lift. He felt freer than he had in a long time.

One day as he wandered through the goldenrod that bordered a thicket, he heard a strange sound. And then he discovered something puzzling and horrible.

riend Hare was thrashing on the ground. A thin rope was twisted around his neck, and the harder the hare struggled the tighter the rope became. The hare was slowly being strangled.

Bambi studied the rope, which was tied to a branch. "Lie still, Friend Hare," he commanded. "I will try to help you."

The hare calmed down. He lay motionless, flat on the ground, his breath rattling in his throat.

Bambi took the branch between his teeth and bent it down. Then he held it to the earth with his hoof and snapped it with a single blow of his antlers. "Now I must get this tight thing off your neck. Lie still and be brave," Bambi gently told the hare as he slipped a prong of his antler under the rope. He drove his antler deeper and deeper under the noose, exerting all his strength.

Finally the noose broke with a loud snap and the hare slipped out and was free.

The poor creature was still so frightened that he instantly hopped off without thanking Bambi. But Bambi understood. He stared at the limp noose and cautiously pawed at it. Just then the old stag stepped out of the thicket. Bambi looked at him and said in a shaken voice, "He isn't here, but still He can kill."

The old stag said bitterly, "How did your Gobo put it? . . . Didn't Gobo say He is all-powerful and all-good?"

"He was good to Gobo," Bambi whispered.

"Do you believe that, Bambi?" the Great Prince asked sadly. For the first time he had called Bambi by his name.

"I don't know," cried Bambi. "I don't understand it."

The old stag said, "We must learn to live and be cautious."

he seasons came and went and Bambi grew into a strong, handsome prince. He was often helped by the old stag, who mysteriously appeared at times when Bambi needed him most. Bambi learned much from the old stag. Once when His fire wounded Bambi's shoulder the old stag led Bambi to a secret hiding place, a hidden hollow under a giant fallen beech, where he could safely lie until his wound healed. The old stag also knew just which weeds Bambi should eat to heal the wound faster. The old stag knew all the ways of the forest.

His head was completely grey now and his face was perfectly gaunt. The deep light in his eyes was faded, and he stayed resting under the fallen beech more frequently. But he was still able to surprise Bambi by suddenly appearing.

One winter day a single crash like thunder rang out. Bambi instinctively ran deeper into the woods, away from the sound of the crash, until suddenly he was met by the old stag.

"Come with me, Bambi, I want to show you something . . . before I go," said the old stag softly.

They had not gone far
when they caught the first whiff
of that sharp ugly smell that sent
dread and terror to their hearts.
Bambi stopped.

"Come. Don't be frightened," said
the old stag.

They kept walking closer and closer
to the terrifying scent. Bambi wanted
to run the other way, but he kept a firm
grip on himself and stayed close behind.

"Here He is," said the old stag.

Through the bare branches, Bambi saw
Him lying on the snow a few steps away.
There was a pool of blood around His head.

"He's lying there dead, like one of us,"
began the old stag. "See, Bambi, He isn't
all-powerful. He isn't above us. He can be
killed like us, and then lies helpless on the
ground like all of us. He's just the same as
we are."

There was a silence. "Do you understand
me, Bambi?" asked the old stag.

Bambi was inspired, and said, trembling,
"There is Another who is over us all, over
us and over Him."

"Now I can go," said the old stag. "Don't
follow me. My time is up. Good-bye, my
son, I loved you dearly."

The years passed. Bambi was now the largest, wisest, and most regal prince in the forest.

He missed the old stag. He lived totally alone now, deep in the forest under the fallen beech tree. But sometimes he would visit the corner of the woods where he had spent his childhood. The great oak was gone – chopped down by Him – but some trails that Bambi and his mother had used were still there.

Once while wandering there he glimpsed Faline and his heart beat faster. She moved slowly, as though she were tired and sad. He wanted to rush to her, to talk to her about their youth and everything that had happened.

He gazed after her as she went off, passing under the bare branches till finally she was lost to sight.

Another time one summer morning he heard the plaintive call of two little fawns. "Mother! Mother!"

Bambi stepped out onto the trail and looked at them sternly. "Can't you stay by yourselves?" he asked.

The little brother and sister were too in awe of the great stag to answer.

Bambi turned and glided into the bushes. *The little fellow pleases me,* he thought. *Perhaps I'll meet him again when he's larger.* He walked along and thought, *The little girl is nice too. Faline looked like that.*

Bambi went on and vanished in the forest.

First published in Great Britain in 2004 by Simon & Schuster UK Ltd
Africa House, 64-78 Kingsway, London WC2B 6AH

Originally published in 1999 by Atheneum Books for Young Readers,
an imprint of Simon & Schuster Children's Publishing Division, New York

Book designed by Lou Fancher
The text for this book is set in Adobe Jenson
The paintings are rendered in oil on paper

A CIP catalogue record for this book is available from the British Library upon request

ISBN 0-689-86074-9
Printed in Italy
1 3 5 7 9 10 8 6 4 2